To Build a Fire

Jack London

DIAMOND BOOKS

Publisher	:	**Diamond Pocket Books (P) Ltd.** X-30, Okhla Industrial Area, Phase-II New Delhi-110020
Phone	:	011- 40712200
E-mail	:	sales@dpb.in
Website	:	www.diamondbook.in

To Build a Fire

By - *Jack London*

About the Author

Jack London was an American novelist and short-story writer. He was one of the most extensively translated of American authors in the 20th century. London's best-known works are: *The Call of the Wild* and *White Fang*. They depict elemental struggles for survival. In the beginning, the author set himself a daily schedule of producing sonnets, ballads, jokes, anecdotes, adventure stories, or horror stories.

His first book, *The Son of the Wolf: Tales of the Far North*, a collection of short stories, gained a wide audience. Later on, to compensate the urgency of writing for money, London wrote *The Cruise of the Snark* in 1911, describing his adventures. He also wrote two autobiographical novels of considerable interest: *The Road* and *John Burleycorn*. Other important novels are *The Sea-Wolf* and *The Iron Heel*.

To Build a Fire

Day had broken cold and grey, exceedingly cold and grey, when the man turned aside from the main Yukon trail and climbed the high earth-bank, where a dim ands little-travelled trail led eastward through the fat spruce timberland.

It was a steep bank, and he paused for breath at the top, excusing the act to himself by looking at his watch.

It was nine o'clock.

There was no sun nor hint of sun, though there was not a cloud in the sky. It was a clear day, and yet there seemed an intangible pall over the face of things, a subtle gloom that made the day dark, and that was due to the absence of sun.

This fact did not worry the man.

He was used to the lack of sun.

It had been days since he had seen the sun, and he knew that a few more days must pass before that cheerful orb, due south, would just peep above the sky-line and dip immediately from view.

The man flung a look back along the way he had come.

The Yukon lay a mile wide and hidden under three feet of ice.

On top of this ice were as many feet of snow.

It was all pure white, rolling in gentle undulations where the ice-jams of the freeze-up had formed.

North and south, as far as his eye could see, it was unbroken white, save for a dark hair-line that curved and twisted from around the spruce-covered island to the south, and that curved and twisted away into the north, where it disappeared behind another spruce-covered island.

This dark hair-line was the trail — the main trail — that led south five hundred miles to the Chilcoot Pass, Dyea, and salt water; and that led north seventy miles to Dawson, and still on to the north a thousand miles to Nulato, and finally to St. Michael on Bering Sea, a thousand miles and half a thousand more.

But all this — the mysterious, far-reaching hairline trail, the absence of sun from the sky, the tremendous cold, and the strangeness and weirdness of it all — made no impression on the man.

It was not because he was long used to it.

He was a new-comer in the land, a chechaquo, and this was his first winter.

The trouble with him was that he was without imagination.

He was quick and alert in the things of life, but only in the things, and not in the significances.

Fifty degrees below zero meant eighty odd degrees of frost.

Such fact impressed him as being cold and uncomfortable, and that was all.

It did not lead him to meditate upon his frailty as a creature of temperature, and upon man's frailty in general, able only to live within certain narrow limits of heat and cold; and from there on it did not lead him to the conjectural field of immortality and man's place in the universe.

Fifty degrees below zero stood for a bite of frost that hurt and that must be guarded against by the use of mittens, ear-flaps, warm moccasins, and thick socks.

Fifty degrees below zero was to him just precisely fifty degrees below zero.

That there should be anything more to it than that was a thought that never entered his head.

As he turned to go on, he spat speculatively.

There was a sharp, explosive crackle that startled him.

He spat again.

And again, in the air, before it could fall to the snow, the spittle crackled.

He knew that at fifty below spittle crackled on the snow, but this spittle had crackled in the air.

Undoubtedly it was colder than fifty below — how much colder he did not know.

But the temperature did not matter.

He was bound for the old claim on the left fork of Henderson Creek, where the boys were already.

They had come over across the divide from the Indian Creek country, while he had come the roundabout way to take a look at the possibilities of getting out logs in the spring from the islands in the Yukon.

He would be in to camp by six o'clock; a bit after dark, it was true, but the boys would be there, a fire would be going, and a hot supper would be ready.

As for lunch, he pressed his hand against the protruding bundle under his jacket. It was also under his shirt, wrapped up in a handkerchief and lying against the naked skin.

It was the only way to keep the biscuits from freezing.

He smiled agreeably to himself as he thought of those biscuits, each cut open and sopped in bacon grease, and each enclosing a generous slice of fried bacon.

He plunged in among the big spruce trees.

The trail was faint.

A foot of snow had fallen since the last sled had passed over, and he was glad he was without a sled, travelling light. In fact, he carried nothing but the lunch wrapped in the handkerchief.

He was surprised, however, at the cold.

It certainly was cold, he concluded, as he rubbed his numbed nose and cheek-bones with his mittened hand.

He was a warm-whiskered man, but the hair on his face did not protect the high cheek-bones and the eager nose that thrust itself aggressively into the frosty air.

At the man's heels trotted a dog, a big native husky, the proper wolf-dog, grey-coated and without any visible or temperamental difference from its brother, the wild wolf.

The animal was depressed by the tremendous cold.

It knew that it was no time for travelling.

Its instinct told it a truer tale than was told to the man by the man's judgment.

In reality, it was not merely colder than fifty below zero; it was colder than sixty below, than seventy below.

It was seventy-five below zero.

Since the freezing-point is thirty-two above zero, it meant that one hundred and seven degrees of frost obtained.

The dog did not know anything about thermometers.

Possibly in its brain there was no sharp consciousness of a condition of very cold such as was in the man's brain.

But the brute had its instinct.

It experienced a vague but menacing apprehension that subdued it and made it slink along at the man's heels, and that made it question eagerly every unwonted movement of the man as if expecting him to go into camp or to seek shelter somewhere and build a fire.

The dog had learned fire, and it wanted fire, or else to burrow under the snow and cuddle its warmth away from the air.

The frozen moisture of its breathing had settled on its fur in a fine powder of frost, and especially were its jowls, muzzle, and eyelashes whitened by its crystalled breath.

The man's red beard and moustache were likewise frosted, but more solidly, the deposit taking the form of ice and increasing with every warm, moist breath he exhaled.

Also, the man was chewing tobacco, and the muzzle of ice held his lips so rigidly that he was unable to clear his chin when he expelled the juice.

The result was that a crystal beard of the colour and solidity of amber was increasing its length on his chin. If he fell down it would shatter itself, like glass, into brittle fragments.

But he did not mind the appendage.

It was the penalty all tobacco-chewers paid in that country, and he had been out before in two cold snaps.

They had not been so cold as this, he knew, but by the spirit thermometer at Sixty Mile he knew they had been registered at fifty below and at fifty-five.

He held on through the level stretch of woods for several miles, crossed a wide flat of nigger-heads, and dropped down a bank to the frozen bed of a small stream.

This was Henderson Creek, and he knew he was ten miles from the forks.

He looked at his watch.

It was ten o'clock.

He was making four miles an hour, and he calculated that he would arrive at the forks at half-past twelve.

He decided to celebrate that event by eating his lunch there.

The dog dropped in again at his heels, with a tail drooping discouragement, as the man swung along the creek-bed.

The furrow of the old sled-trail was plainly visible, but a dozen inches of snow covered the marks of the last runners.

In a month no man had come up or down that silent creek.

The man held steadily on.

He was not much given to thinking, and just then particularly he had nothing to think about save that he would eat lunch at the forks and that at six o'clock he would be in camp with the boys.

There was nobody to talk to and, had there been, speech would have been impossible because of the ice-muzzle on his mouth.

So he continued monotonously to chew tobacco and to increase the length of his amber beard.

Once in a while the thought reiterated itself that it was very cold and that he had never experienced such cold.

As he walked along he rubbed his cheek-bones and nose with the back of his mittened hand.

He did this automatically, now and again changing hands.

But rub as he would, the instant he stopped his cheek-bones went numb, and the following instant the end of his nose went numb.

He was sure to frost his cheeks; he knew that, and experienced a pang of regret that he had not devised a nose-strap of the sort Bud wore in cold snaps.

Such a strap passed across the cheeks, as well, and saved them.

But it didn't matter much, after all.

What were frosted cheeks?

A bit painful, that was all; they were never serious.

Empty as the man's mind was of thoughts, he was keenly observant, and he noticed the changes in the creek, the curves and bends and timber-jams, and always he sharply noted where he placed his feet.

Once, coming around a bend, he shied abruptly, like a startled horse, curved away from the place where he had been walking, and retreated several paces back along the trail.

The creek he knew was frozen clear to the bottom — no creek could contain water in that arctic winter — but he knew also that there were springs that bubbled out from the hillsides and ran along under the snow and on top the ice of the creek.

He knew that the coldest snaps never froze these springs, and he knew likewise their danger.

They were traps.

They hid pools of water under the snow that might be three inches deep, or three feet.

Sometimes a skin of ice half an inch thick covered them, and in turn was covered by the snow.

Sometimes there were alternate layers of water and ice-skin, so that when one broke through he kept on breaking through for a while, sometimes wetting himself to the waist.

That was why he had shied in such panic.

He had felt the give under his feet and heard the crackle of a snow-hidden ice-skin.

And to get his feet wet in such a temperature meant trouble and danger.

At the very least it meant delay, for he would be forced to stop and build a fire, and under its protection to bare his feet while he dried his socks and moccasins.

He stood and studied the creek-bed and its banks, and decided that the flow of water came from the right.

He reflected awhile, rubbing his nose and cheeks, then skirted to the left, stepping gingerly and testing the footing for each step.

Once clear of the danger, he took a fresh chew of tobacco and swung along at his four-mile gait.

In the course of the next two hours he came upon several similar traps.

Usually the snow above the hidden pools had a sunken, candied appearance that advertised the danger.

Once again, however, he had a close call; and once, suspecting danger, he compelled the dog to go on in front.

The dog did not want to go.

It hung back until the man shoved it forward, and then it went quickly across the white, unbroken surface.

Suddenly it broke through, floundered to one side, and got away to firmer footing.

It had wet its forefeet and legs, and almost immediately the water that clung to it turned to ice.

It made quick efforts to lick the ice off its legs, then dropped down in the snow and began to bite out the ice that had formed between the toes.

This was a matter of instinct.

To permit the ice to remain would mean sore feet.

It did not know this. It merely obeyed the mysterious prompting that arose from the deep crypts of its being.

But the man knew, having achieved a judgment on the subject, and he removed the mitten from his right hand and helped tear out the ice-particles.

He did not expose his fingers more than a minute, and was astonished at the swift numbness that smote them.

It certainly was cold.

He pulled on the mitten hastily, and beat the hand savagely across his chest.

At twelve o'clock the day was at its brightest.

Yet the sun was too far south on its winter journey to clear the horizon.

The bulge of the earth intervened between it and Henderson Creek, where the man walked under a clear sky at noon and cast no shadow.

At half-past twelve, to the minute, he arrived at the forks of the creek.

He was pleased at the speed he had made.

If he kept it up, he would certainly be with the boys by six.

He unbuttoned his jacket and shirt and drew forth his lunch.

The action consumed no more than a quarter of a minute, yet in that brief moment the numbness laid hold of the exposed fingers.

He did not put the mitten on, but, instead, struck the fingers a dozen sharp smashes against his leg.

Then he sat down on a snow-covered log to eat.

The sting that followed upon the striking of his fingers against his leg ceased so quickly that he was startled, he had had no chance to take a bite of biscuit.

He struck the fingers repeatedly and returned them to the mitten, baring the other hand for the purpose of eating.

He tried to take a mouthful, but the ice-muzzle prevented.

He had forgotten to build a fire and thaw out.

He chuckled at his foolishness, and as he chuckled he noted the numbness creeping into the exposed fingers.

Also, he noted that the stinging which had first come to his toes when he sat down was already passing away.

He wondered whether the toes were warm or numbed.

He moved them inside the moccasins and decided that they were numbed.

He pulled the mitten on hurriedly and stood up. He was a bit frightened.

He stamped up and down until the stinging returned into the feet.

It certainly was cold, was his thought.

That man from Sulphur Creek had spoken the truth when telling how cold it sometimes got in the country.

And he had laughed at him at the time!

That showed one must not be too sure of things.

There was no mistake about it, it was cold.

He strode up and down, stamping his feet and threshing his arms, until reassured by the returning warmth.

Then he got out matches and proceeded to make a fire.

From the undergrowth, where high water of the previous spring had lodged a supply of seasoned twigs, he got his firewood.

Working carefully from a small beginning, he soon had a roaring fire, over which he thawed the ice from his face and in the protection of which he ate his biscuits.

For the moment the cold of space was outwitted.

The dog took satisfaction in the fire, stretching out close enough for warmth and far enough away to escape being singed.

When the man had finished, he filled his pipe and took his comfortable time over a smoke.

Then he pulled on his mittens, settled the ear-flaps of his cap firmly about his ears, and took the creek trail up the left fork.

The dog was disappointed and yearned back toward the fire.

This man did not know cold.

Possibly all the generations of his ancestry had been ignorant of cold, of real cold, of cold one hundred and seven degrees below freezing-point.

But the dog knew; all its ancestry knew, and it had inherited the knowledge.

And it knew that it was not good to walk abroad in such fearful cold.

It was the time to lie snug in a hole in the snow and wait for a curtain of cloud to be drawn across the face of outer space whence this cold came.

On the other hand, there was keen intimacy between the dog and the man.

The one was the toil-slave of the other, and the only caresses it had ever received were the caresses of the whip-lash and of harsh and menacing throat-sounds that threatened the whip-lash.

So the dog made no effort to communicate its apprehension to the man.

It was not concerned in the welfare of the man; it was for its own sake that it yearned back toward the fire.

But the man whistled, and spoke to it with the sound of whip-lashes, and the dog swung in at the man's heels and followed after.

The man took a chew of tobacco and proceeded to start a new amber beard.

Also, his moist breath quickly powdered with white his moustache, eyebrows, and lashes.

There did not seem to be so many springs on the left fork of the Henderson, and for half an hour the man saw no signs of any.

And then it happened.

At a place where there were no signs, where the soft, unbroken snow seemed to advertise solidity beneath, the man broke through.

It was not deep.

He wetted himself half-way to the knees before he floundered out to the firm crust.

He was angry, and cursed his luck aloud.

He had hoped to get into camp with the boys at six o'clock, and this would delay him an hour, for he would have to build a fire and dry out his footgear.

This was imperative at that low temperature — he knew that much; and he turned aside to the bank, which he climbed.

On top, tangled in the underbrush about the trunks of several small spruce trees, was a high-water deposit of dry firewood — sticks and twigs principally, but also larger portions of seasoned branches and fine, dry, last-year's grasses.

He threw down several large pieces on top of the snow. This served for a foundation and prevented the young flame from drowning itself in the snow it otherwise would melt.

The flame he got by touching a match to a small shred of birch-bark that he took from his pocket.

This burned even more readily than paper.

Placing it on the foundation, he fed the young flame with wisps of dry grass and with the tiniest dry twigs.

He worked slowly and carefully, keenly aware of his danger.

Gradually, as the flame grew stronger, he increased the size of the twigs with which he fed it.

He squatted in the snow, pulling the twigs out from their entanglement in the brush and feeding directly to the flame.

He knew there must be no failure.

When it is seventy-five below zero, a man must not fail in his first attempt to build a fire — that is, if his feet are wet.

If his feet are dry, and he fails, he can run along the trail for half a mile and restore his circulation.

But the circulation of wet and freezing feet cannot be restored by running when it is seventy-five below.

No matter how fast he runs, the wet feet will freeze the harder.

All this the man knew.

The old-timer on Sulphur Creek had told him about it the previous fall, and now he was appreciating the advice.

Already all sensation had gone out of his feet.

To build the fire he had been forced to remove his mittens, and the fingers had quickly gone numb.

His pace of four miles an hour had kept his heart pumping blood to the surface of his body and to all the extremities.

But the instant he stopped, the action of the pump eased down.

The cold of space smote the unprotected tip of the planet, and he, being on that unprotected tip, received the full force of the blow.

The blood of his body recoiled before it.

The blood was alive, like the dog, and like the dog it wanted to hide away and cover itself up from the fearful cold.

So long as he walked four miles an hour, he pumped that blood, willy-nilly, to the surface; but now it ebbed away and sank down into the recesses of his body.

The extremities were the first to feel its absence.

His wet feet froze the faster, and his exposed fingers numbed the faster, though they had not yet begun to freeze.

Nose and cheeks were already freezing, while the skin of all his body chilled as it lost its blood.

But he was safe.

Toes and nose and cheeks would be only touched by the frost, for the fire was beginning to burn with strength.

He was feeding it with twigs the size of his finger.

In another minute he would be able to feed it with branches the size of his wrist, and then he could remove his wet foot-gear, and, while it dried, he could keep his naked feet warm by the fire, rubbing them at first, of course, with snow.

The fire was a success.

He was safe.

He remembered the advice of the old-timer on Sulphur Creek, and smiled.

The old-timer had been very serious in laying down the law that no man must travel alone in the Klondike after fifty below.

Well, here he was; he had had the accident; he was alone; and he had saved himself.

Those old-timers were rather womanish, some of them, he thought.

All a man had to do was to keep his head, and he was all right.

Any man who was a man could travel alone.

But it was surprising, the rapidity with which his cheeks and nose were freezing.

And he had not thought his fingers could go lifeless in so short a time.

Lifeless they were, for he could scarcely make them move together to grip a twig, and they seemed remote from his body and from him.

When he touched a twig, he had to look and see whether or not he had hold of it.

The wires were pretty well down between him and his finger-ends.

All of which counted for little.

There was the fire, snapping and crackling and promising life with every dancing flame.

He started to untie his moccasins.

They were coated with ice; the thick German socks were like sheaths of iron half-way to the knees; and the mocassin strings were like rods of steel all twisted and knotted as by some conflagration.

For a moment he tugged with his numbed fingers, then, realizing the folly of it, he drew his sheath-knife.

But before he could cut the strings, it happened.

It was his own fault or, rather, his mistake.

He should not have built the fire under the spruce tree.

He should have built it in the open.

But it had been easier to pull the twigs from the brush and drop them directly on the fire.

Now the tree under which he had done this carried a weight of snow on its boughs.

No wind had blown for weeks, and each bough was fully freighted.

Each time he had pulled a twig he had communicated a slight agitation to the tree — an imperceptible agitation, so far as he was concerned, but an agitation sufficient to bring about the disaster.

High up in the tree one bough capsized its load of snow.

This fell on the boughs beneath, capsizing them.

This process continued, spreading out and involving the whole tree.

It grew like an avalanche, and it descended without warning upon the man and the fire, and the fire was blotted out!

Where it had burned was a mantle of fresh and disordered snow.

The man was shocked.

It was as though he had just heard his own sentence of death.

For a moment he sat and stared at the spot where the fire had been.

Then he grew very calm.

Perhaps the old-timer on Sulphur Creek was right.

If he had only had a trail-mate he would have been in no danger now. The trail-mate could have built the fire.

Well, it was up to him to build the fire over again, and this second time there must be no failure.

Even if he succeeded, he would most likely lose some toes.

His feet must be badly frozen by now, and there would be some time before the second fire was ready.

Such were his thoughts, but he did not sit and think them.

He was busy all the time they were passing through his mind, he made a new foundation for a fire, this time in the open; where no treacherous tree could blot it out.

Next, he gathered dry grasses and tiny twigs from the high-water flotsam.

He could not bring his fingers together to pull them out, but he was able to gather them by the handful.

In this way he got many rotten twigs and bits of green moss that were undesirable, but it was the best he could do.

He worked methodically, even collecting an armful of the larger branches to be used later when the fire gathered strength.

And all the while the dog sat and watched him, a certain yearning wistfulness in its eyes, for it looked upon him as the fire-provider, and the fire was slow in coming.

When all was ready, the man reached in his pocket for a second piece of birch-bark.

He knew the bark was there, and, though he could not feel it with his fingers, he could hear its crisp rustling as he fumbled for it.

Try as he would, he could not clutch hold of it.

And all the time, in his consciousness, was the knowledge that each instant his feet were freezing.

This thought tended to put him in a panic, but he fought against it and kept calm.

He pulled on his mittens with his teeth, and threshed his arms back and forth, beating his hands with all his might against his sides. He did this sitting down, and he stood up to do it; and all the while the dog sat in the snow, its wolf-brush of a tail curled around warmly over its forefeet, its sharp wolf-ears pricked forward intently as it watched the man.

And the man as he beat and threshed with his arms and hands, felt a great surge of envy as he regarded the creature that was warm and secure in its natural covering.

After a time he was aware of the first far-away signals of sensation in his beaten fingers.

The faint tingling grew stronger till it evolved into a stinging ache that was excruciating, but which the man hailed with satisfaction.

He stripped the mitten from his right hand and fetched forth the birch-bark.

The exposed fingers were quickly going numb again.

Next he brought out his bunch of sulphur matches.

But the tremendous cold had already driven the life out of his fingers.

In his effort to separate one match from the others, the whole bunch fell in the snow.

He tried to pick it out of the snow, but failed.

The dead fingers could neither touch nor clutch.

He was very careful.

He drove the thought of his freezing feet; and nose, and cheeks, out of his mind, devoting his whole soul to the matches.

He watched, using the sense of vision in place of that of touch, and when he saw his fingers on each side the bunch, he closed them — that is, he willed to close them, for the wires were drawn, and the fingers did not obey.

He pulled the mitten on the right hand, and beat it fiercely against his knee.

Then, with both mittened hands, he scooped the bunch of matches, along with much snow, into his lap.

Yet he was no better off.

After some manipulation he managed to get the bunch between the heels of his mittened hands. In this fashion he carried it to his mouth.

The ice crackled and snapped when by a violent effort he opened his mouth.

He drew the lower jaw in, curled the upper lip out of the way, and scraped the bunch with his upper teeth in order to separate a match.

He succeeded in getting one, which he dropped on his lap.

He was no better off.

He could not pick it up.

Then he devised a way.

He picked it up in his teeth and scratched it on his leg.

Twenty times he scratched before he succeeded in lighting it.

As it flamed he held it with his teeth to the birch-bark.

But the burning brimstone went up his nostrils and into his lungs, causing him to cough spasmodically.

The match fell into the snow and went out.

The old-timer on Sulphur Creek was right, he thought in the moment of controlled despair that ensued: after fifty below, a man should travel with a partner.

He beat his hands, but failed in exciting any sensation.

Suddenly he bared both hands, removing the mittens with his teeth.

He caught the whole bunch between the heels of his hands.

His arm-muscles not being frozen enabled him to press the hand-heels tightly against the matches.

Then he scratched the bunch along his leg.

It flared into flame, seventy sulphur matches at once!

There was no wind to blow them out.

He kept his head to one side to escape the strangling fumes, and held the blazing bunch to the birch-bark.

As he so held it, he became aware of sensation in his hand.

His flesh was burning. He could smell it.

Deep down below the surface he could feel it.

The sensation developed into pain that grew acute.

And still he endured it, holding the flame of the matches clumsily to the bark that would not light readily because his own burning hands were in the way, absorbing most of the flame.

At last, when he could endure no more, he jerked his hands apart.

The blazing matches fell sizzling into the snow, but the birch-bark was alight.

He began laying dry grasses and the tiniest twigs on the flame.

He could not pick and choose, for he had to lift the fuel between the heels of his hands.

Small pieces of rotten wood and green moss clung to the twigs, and he bit them off as well as he could with his teeth.

He cherished the flame carefully and awkwardly.

It meant life, and it must not perish.

The withdrawal of blood from the surface of his body now made him begin to shiver, and he grew more awkward.

A large piece of green moss fell squarely on the little fire.

He tried to poke it out with his fingers, but his shivering frame made him poke too far, and he disrupted the nucleus of the little fire, the burning grasses and tiny twigs separating and scattering.

He tried to poke them together again, but in spite of the tenseness of the effort, his shivering got away with him, and the twigs were hopelessly scattered.

Each twig gushed a puff of smoke and went out.

The fire-provider had failed.

As he looked apathetically about him, his eyes chanced on the dog, sitting across the ruins of the fire from him, in the snow, making restless, hunching movements, slightly lifting one forefoot and then the other, shifting its weight back and forth on them with wistful eagerness.

The sight of the dog put a wild idea into his head.

He remembered the tale of the man, caught in a blizzard, who killed a steer and crawled inside the carcass, and so was saved.

He would kill the dog and bury his hands in the warm body until the numbness went out of them.

Then he could build another fire.

He spoke to the dog, calling it to him; but in his voice was a strange note of fear that frightened the animal, who had never known the man to speak in such way before.

Something was the matter, and its suspicious nature sensed danger, — it knew not what danger but somewhere, somehow, in its brain arose an apprehension of the man.

It flattened its ears down at the sound of the man's voice, and its restless, hunching movements and the liftings and shiftings of its forefeet became more pronounced but it would not come to the man.

He got on his hands and knees and crawled toward the dog.

This unusual posture again excited suspicion, and the animal sidled mincingly away.

The man sat up in the snow for a moment and struggled for calmness.

Then he pulled on his mittens, by means of his teeth, and got upon his feet.

He glanced down at first in order to assure himself that he was really standing up, for the absence of sensation in his feet left him unrelated to the earth.

His erect position in itself started to drive the webs of suspicion from the dog's mind; and when he spoke peremptorily, with the sound of whip-lashes in his voice, the dog rendered its customary allegiance and came to him.

As it came within reaching distance, the man lost his control.

His arms flashed out to the dog, and he experienced genuine surprise when he discovered that his hands could not clutch, that there was neither bend nor feeling in the lingers.

He had forgotten for the moment that they were frozen and that they were freezing more and more.

All this happened quickly, and before the animal could get away, he encircled its body with his arms.

He sat down in the snow, and in this fashion held the dog, while it snarled and whined and struggled.

But it was all he could do, hold its body encircled in his arms and sit there.

He realized that he could not kill the dog.

There was no way to do it.

With his helpless hands he could neither draw nor hold his sheath-knife nor throttle the animal.

He released it, and it plunged wildly away, with tail between its legs, and still snarling.

It halted forty feet away and surveyed him curiously, with ears sharply pricked forward.

The man looked down at his hands in order to locate them, and found them hanging on the ends of his arms.

It struck him as curious that one should have to use his eyes in order to find out where his hands were.

He began threshing his arms back and forth, beating the mittened hands against his sides.

He did this for five minutes, violently, and his heart pumped enough blood up to the surface to put a stop to his shivering.

But no sensation was aroused in the hands. He had an impression that they hung like weights on the ends of his arms, but when he tried to run the impression down, he could not find it.

A certain fear of death, dull and oppressive, came to him.

This fear quickly became poignant as he realized that it was no longer a mere matter of freezing his fingers and toes, or of losing his hands and feet, but that it was a matter of life and death with the chances against him.

This threw him into a panic, and he turned and ran up the creek-bed along the old, dim trail.

The dog joined in behind and kept up with him.

He ran blindly, without intention, in fear such as he had never known in his life.

Slowly, as he ploughed and floundered through the snow, he began to see things again — the banks of the creek, the old timber-jams, the leafless aspens, and the sky.

The running made him feel better.

He did not shiver.

Maybe, if he ran on, his feet would thaw out; and, anyway, if he ran far enough, he would reach camp and the boys.

Without doubt he would lose some fingers and toes and some of his face; but the boys would take care of him, and save the rest of him when he got there.

And at the same time there was another thought in his mind that said he would never get to the camp and the boys; that it was too many miles away, that the freezing had too great a start on him, and that he would soon be stiff and dead.

This thought he kept in the background and refused to consider.

Sometimes it pushed itself forward and demanded to be heard, but he thrust it back and strove to think of other things.

It struck him as curious that he could run at all on feet so frozen that he could not feel them when they struck the earth and took the weight of his body.

He seemed to himself to skim along above the surface and to have no connection with the earth.

Somewhere he had once seen a winged Mercury, and he wondered if Mercury felt as he felt when skimming over the earth.

His theory of running until he reached camp and the boys had one flaw in it: he lacked the endurance.

Several times he stumbled, and finally he tottered, crumpled up, and fell.

When he tried to rise, he failed.

He must sit and rest, he decided, and next time he would merely walk and keep on going.

As he sat and regained his breath, he noted that he was feeling quite warm and comfortable.

He was not shivering, and it even seemed that a warm glow had come to his chest and trunk.

And yet, when he touched his nose or cheeks, there was no sensation.

Running would not thaw them out. Nor would it thaw out his hands and feet.

Then the thought came to him that the frozen portions of his body must be extending.

He tried to keep this thought down, to forget it, to think of something else; he was aware of the panicky feeling that it caused, and he was afraid of the panic.

But the thought asserted itself, and persisted, until it produced a vision of his body totally frozen.

This was too much, and he made another wild run along the trail.

Once he slowed down to a walk, but the thought of the freezing extending itself made him run again.

And all the time the dog ran with him, at his heels.

When he fell down a second time, it curled its tail over its forefeet and sat in front of him facing him curiously eager and intent.

The warmth and security of the animal angered him, and he cursed it till it flattened down its ears appeasingly.

This time the shivering came more quickly upon the man.

He was losing in his battle with the frost. It was creeping into his body from all sides.

The thought of it drove him on, but he ran no more than a hundred feet, when he staggered and pitched headlong.

It was his last panic.

When he had recovered his breath and control, he sat up and entertained in his mind the conception of meeting death with dignity.

However, the conception did not come to him in such terms.

His idea of it was that he had been making a fool of himself, running around like a chicken with its head cut off — such was the simile that occurred to him.

Well, he was bound to freeze anyway, and he might as well take it decently.

With this new-found peace of mind came the first glimmerings of drowsiness.

A good idea, he thought, to sleep off to death.

It was like taking an anæsthetic.

Freezing was not so bad as people thought.

There were lots worse ways to die.

He pictured the boys finding his body next day. Suddenly he found himself with them, coming along the trail and looking for himself.

And, still with them, he came around a turn in the trail and found himself lying in the snow.

He did not belong with himself any more, for even then he was out of himself, standing with the boys and looking at himself in the snow.

It certainly was cold, was his thought.

When he got back to the States he could tell the folks what real cold was.

He drifted on from this to a vision of the old-timer on Sulphur Creek.

He could see him quite clearly, warm and comfortable, and smoking a pipe.

"You were right, old hoss; you were right," the man mumbled to the old-timer of Sulphur Creek.

Then the man drowsed off into what seemed to him the most comfortable and satisfying sleep he had ever known.

The dog sat facing him and waiting.

The brief day drew to a close in a long, slow twilight.

There were no signs of a fire to be made, and, besides, never in the dog's experience had it known a man to sit like that in the snow and make no fire.

As the twilight drew on, its eager yearning for the fire mastered it, and with a great lifting and shifting of forefeet, it whined softly, then flattened its ears down in anticipation of being chidden by the man.

But the man remained silent.

Later, the dog whined loudly.

And still later it crept close to the man and caught the scent of death.

This made the animal bristle and back away.

A little longer it delayed, howling under the stars that leaped and danced and shone brightly in the cold sky.

Then it turned and trotted up the trail in the direction of the camp it knew, where were the other food-providers and fire-providers.

***